The troll boy and the witch
Idea and text: Erik Arpi
Illustrations: Garcia Arias and Juan Vernet
An original production by Pictura Normann A.S., Norway
Print and original work: Haslum Grafisk AS, 2005
Translated by: Language Power Center, Oslo

The troll boy and the witch

Idea and text: Erik Arpi

Illustrations: Garcia Arias and Juan Vernet

Normann
NORMANNS KUNSTFORLAG

Once upon a time, long before the humans existed, the earth was covered with huge forests, so deep that if you tried to enter them, you would probably never find your way out again.

In these forests there were wild animals, but also different kinds of witches, elves and trolls. The trolls lived in small villages often far from each other.

In one of the villages lived a little troll boy called Jonte. Jonte was a nice troll and he was hardly afraid of anything.

In the same village lived a young troll girl called Malva. She had a laugh which made everyone around her laugh. Jonte and Malva were very fond of each other and had decided that they wanted to get married. Malva's dad was a blacksmith and could make things out of metal. One day he said to Jonte and Malva: "I have something I want to give you". Then he pulled out two shiny gold rings, one smaller than the other. The rings were carefully made so that the small one fitted inside the big one perfectly.

"If something dangerous ever threatens you", he said and gave the small ring to Malva and the big one to Jonte, "just cover the small ring with the big one and no evil will ever harm you. This is because I have put into these rings all the love that your mother and I have shared together throughout a long and wonderful life".

In a mountain, in the darkest and most depressing part of the forest, lived a dangerous and evil witch. She hated happy trolls. They made her feel really bad. However if she saw someone crying, she immediately felt happy. When the witch saw Malva and Jonte walking around in the forest laughing, she almost felt sick.

The day of Malva and Jonte's wedding, Jonte went into the forest to pick some flowers for Malva's wedding bouquet. In the forest he met an old troll woman.

"What is a young troll boy like you doing out in the forest?" the old troll woman asked.

"I am picking flowers for a wedding bouquet", said Jonte.

"Really? That is awful", said the old woman, "well, you shall have to try one of my tasty wild strawberries then".

Jonte didn't really want to try the strawberries, but at the same time he didn't want to offend the old woman; so he took a couple. They tasted strange. Suddenly, everything went dark.

When Jonte woke up, it was almost dark outside. The old troll woman was gone and he had no idea where he was.

The wild strawberries had poisoned him so badly that he couldn't find his way home.

For several weeks, Jonte wandered all over the forest. It had started to snow and Jonte did not know which way to go. And in the mountain, the witch was laughing.

In the end Jonte was so fed up that he just wanted to die. He was so tired that he threw himself on the ground and wished that he would never wake up again.

Then suddenly he heard a voice asking, "why are you lying here?"

"Because I want to die of course", Jonte said with a tired voice.

Suddenly he realized that someone had actually spoken to him and he jumped up!

Not far away from him he saw an unknown troll girl.

"Where do you come from?" Jonte asked.

"From the village", said the troll girl, "but where do you come from?"

"From the village", answered Jonte.

"Well, not from my village, that's for sure", said the girl.

"Do you know where my village is then?" Jonte asked.

"No", said the girl, "but it has to be somewhere far away, as I have never heard of it".

"Never heard of it?" Jonte said sadly.

"No", confirmed the girl.

So Jonte followed the unknown troll girl back to her village. The excitement in the village was huge. All the trolls gathered around Jonte to get a look at him. Nobody had ever seen a troll from another village before.

In spite of Jonte having asked all the trolls, no one had heard of the village he came from. But the trolls were very hospitable and curious and in the end they asked Jonte if he wanted to stay in their village.

What could he do? In reality, all he wanted was to go back to Malva.

"But if I go back into the forest, I will just get lost and die and I don't want that to happen", he thought to himself. "So the best thing is probably for me to stay here for a while. But as soon as I get a hold of that witch, I will make her show me the way home and then after that I will tie a knot on her long nose, throw her up in the nearest tree and leave her stuck there".

Winter came, spring and summer and autumn, and then winter again, but Jonte hadn't seen any sign of the witch.

After many years, he married the girl who had found him in the forest. But he could never forget Malva.

After a while they had a son who they called Jon. It was a boy who was so similar to his father that the only difference was the age.

When Jonte failed to return to his village, the trolls got worried and went out to look for him. But they couldn't find him anywhere. Malva got so upset that the trolls thought she would die. Her laughter, which had made everyone in the village so happy, could not be heard anymore. It was a sad time for the trolls in the village.

"He will be back again you'll see", they all said to comfort Malva.

But time went by and Jonte was nowhere to be seen.

After many years Malva married another troll boy. But she could never forget about Jonte.

After a while they had a daughter who they called Marja. She was like a miniature of her mother and she also had the same cheerful laugh as her mum once had.

"Finally", said the trolls, "finally someone can make us happy again".

One evening, Jonte told Jon a strange story.

"Well you see", Jonte said, "I am actually from another troll village, far away from here. There I once knew a troll girl called Malva. This girl had a laugh that would make everyone around her happy".

Then he continued telling Jon about the wedding bouquet and the troll woman and of the poisoned strawberries. Jon listened enthusiastically. This was the most exciting story he had ever heard.

At the end of the story Jonte pulled out a gold ring.

"Look at this", he said to Jon. "There is a gold ring which fits perfectly inside this one. If you pull this ring over the small one, no evil can happen to anyone carrying the rings".

"Take this", he said and gave the ring to Jon. "Maybe one day you will find the ring which will fit inside".

"You know, father?" Jon said. "I will find the way to your village".

"But be careful", Jonte said. "The witch in Dark Mountain will go crazy if she sees someone happy and cheerful".

"I can take care of myself", said Jon.

The next day, Jon packed his rucksack and said goodbye to all the trolls in the village. "Do you have to go?" his mother said with tears in her eyes. "What if you go through the same thing as your father did?"

"Don't worry, mother. I can take care of myself", said Jon and went off in the same direction as his father once had arrived.

After he had walked all day and the evening arrived, he heard a voice calling out for help. Jon ran towards the sound of the voice. Soon he realized that the shouts came from a small bear. It had got stuck in a branch, hanging off a cliff. The branch was not thick enough for Jon to climb, but in the end he was able to bend the branch and free the little bear which instantly disappeared into the forest.

It was almost dark and Jon felt tired. He went to lie down, pulled a blanket around himself and fell asleep under a tree.

The first thing Jon saw when he opened his eyes were two huge, yellow eyes staring at him in the twilight.

"It has to be the witch", Jon thought to himself. His heart was beating like mad.

"This is it! Now!"

"What's a troll like you doing out here in the forest at this time of night", said a voice.

Jon could now hear that it was only the voice of an owl.

"You really scared me, owl", said Jon. "Well, I'm looking for my father's village. Could you tell me which way to go?"

"No", said the owl.

"But haven't you heard the story of the troll boy who wandered for ages around the forest after being poisoned by a witch?"

"Hmm", said the owl, "but that was many years ago".

"Yes that's right", said Jon. "But do you know where I can find the village he came from?"

"If you walk directly towards the rising sun", said the owl, "you will find it".

"Is it far?" Jon asked.

"Yes, it will probably take you about twooo….."

Just as the sun came up, the owl immediately fell asleep, as owls tend to do at sunrise.

"She probably meant two hours or two days", Jon thought to himself.

Then he started walking towards the rising sun.

After Jon had been walking for a week, he was really fed up with eating mushrooms, berries and roots. "How far away is this troll village?"

"I wonder if I can even find my way home?" he thought.

He continued for another week and at this point he was extremely fed up with mushrooms, berries and roots. "If I survive this, I will never eat mushrooms again", he thought.

He had been walking for two weeks, but had not yet found a troll village. "What if the owl meant to say two years?"

"How stupid can you get?" Jon thought. "Why didn't I just stay at home with my mother and father?"

Angry, he took his rucksack off and threw it on the ground.

Then suddenly he heard someone laughing behind him.

"Could it be the witch?" he thought and turned around to see.

Just a few steps away from him he saw a little troll girl laughing so cheerfully that he himself felt like laughing.

"What's your name?" Jon asked.

"Marja", the girl answered. "But where do you come from?"

"From a village far away from here", said Jon, "but is there a village near here as well?"

"Yes, just follow me and I'll take you there", said the girl.

Marja and Jon wandered through the forest, chatting and laughing on their way to Marja's village.

Suddenly, an evil creature appeared and blocked their path.

"Well, there you are again", the creature said. "I've had enough of this laughing and happiness. I will transform you into snakes!"

Then the witch lifted her arms and started mumbling some kind of evil troll spell. That's when Jon could see the ring! The ring on the girl's finger. It looked exactly like the one his father had given him.

As fast as he could, he pulled off his ring and pushed it over the girl's ring.

It was as if the witch received an electric shock. She was thrown backwards and then escaped into the forest screaming.

When Marja and Jon arrived in the troll village, all the trolls gathered around them and stared curiously at Jon.

When Marja's mother saw Jon, she suddenly went pale and couldn't say a word.

In the end she finally said: "you look so much like your father".

"You have to be Malva?" Jon said.

"How do you know?" Malva asked astonished.

"My father has told me about you", Jon said.

Suddenly Malva started laughing for the first time in many, many years.

"Where can I find Dark Mountain?" Jon continued.

"Too close", said one of the older trolls. "Nobody wants to go there".

"Yes", said Jon, "I have to go there and chase away the witch once and for all so that we trolls can be happy and cheerful again".

"But think about what happened to your father", said Malva.

"If I take both rings with me, the witch won't be able to hurt me", said Jon.

"I'm coming with you", said Marja.

"But be careful", continued Malva.

"We can take care of ourselves", said Jon.

Next morning, Jon woke up at the sound of someone laughing. It was Marja. "Do you know that you look like a mole when you're sleeping", she said. "But you have to wake up now if we are going to chase the witch away".

They packed some food in Jon's rucksack and headed out.

They had walked for half a day when they arrived at Dark Mountain.

The mountain was almost black and down by the foot, half hidden behind a couple of dark, thin branches, they could see the entrance to the witch's cave. Jon pulled his ring over Marja's and entered the cave.

Inside the cave the witch was sitting by the fire. When she heard the trolls she quickly turned around.

"There you are again", she screamed harshly.

Then she felt the power from the rings and started spitting and frothing.

"Disappear from here now", Marja shouted. "You have caused enough misery around here".

"Misery", the witch screamed, "misery is good".

"Disappear", Jon shouted, "or else…"

Just then, Jon tripped on a rock, dropped the ring and it rolled in front of the witch.

"Ha, ha, ha", laughed the witch and picked up the ring. "That's better! Now I will finally transform you into snakes!"

Suddenly they heard a roar, even worse than the sound of the witch herself. Marja and Jon turned around in fear. Heading towards them was a huge, roaring bear. On its way it pushed over rocks as if they were made out of cork.

"This is just getting worse and worse", screamed Marja.

But the huge bear continued past the terrified trolls, grabbed the witch and threw her out of the cave and into the endlessly deep pond by the foot of the mountain. The witch sank like a rock and since then nobody has ever seen her again.

Then the bear turned towards the trolls.

"Now it's probably our turn", Jon said to Marja. "Can you swim?"

But the big bear just stood there and looked at Jon with a friendly face and said: "This was just a little thank you for saving my baby bear".

Then he turned around and went off.

So what happened to Marja and Jon in the end?

Well, one day, the following summer, Jon went into the forest to pick some flowers for Marja's wedding bouquet. Marja and Jon had decided to get married. So in the end, there was a wedding after all! All the trolls in the village were invited. But Jon had also gone to get his mother and father.

Finally, Malva and Jonte would meet again. But now it was their children who were getting married. And you can just imagine what a wedding it was!

But when Jon was about to put the ring on Marja's finger, he remembered that he himself didn't have a ring anymore. The witch had taken his ring with her into the pond. So what could he do?

That's when Marja's grandfather came to Jon. He was the one who had made the rings. He was old now. Slowly he took out a gold ring and gave it to Jon.

"I made one extra", he said slowly.

Carefully, Jon put the ring on his finger.

Then he got an idea. Quickly he pulled the ring off his finger again and tried it on top of Marja's ring.

"It fits perfectly", said Marja pleased.

"Yes, it certainly does", said Marja's grandfather and laughed.

That's when Marja and Jon felt the power. The most amazing power which comes from the one true love. The one that survives it all!